Long, long ago –
     and very high up –
there lived a kitten.

He was tiny.

ENORMOUSE!

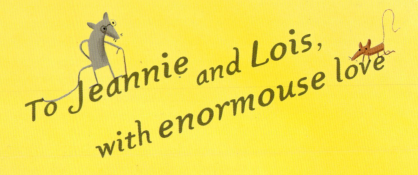

To Jeannie and Lois, with enormouse love

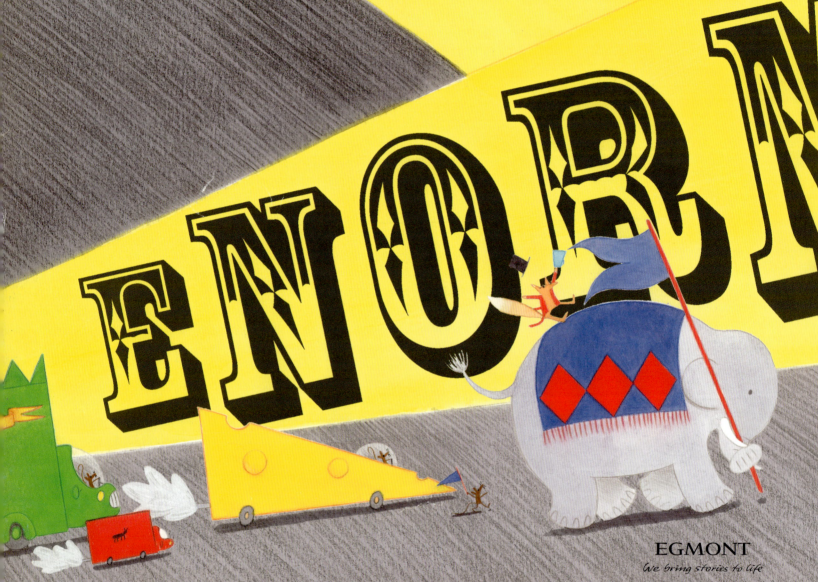

EGMONT
We bring stories to life

First published in Great Britain 2011 by Egmont UK Limited, 239 Kensington High Street, London W8 6SA

Text and illustrations copyright © Rebecca Gerlings 2011

The moral rights of the author/illustrator have been asserted

ISBN 978 1405 2 4831 0 (Hardback)
ISBN 978 1405 2 4832 7 (Paperback)

1 2 3 4 5 6 7 8 9 10

A CIP catalogue record for this title is available from the British Library

Printed and bound in Singapore

But he had
BIG *ideas.*

One day,
the kitten
discovered
it took
just one
BIG idea

to get him
out of the window

and down . . .

down . . .

down . . .

into . . .

A caravan filled
with creatures.

Wild creatures.

Circus creatures.

Mitzy™
Top-notch
cat food

And, luckily,
friendly
creatures . . .

who offered
the kitten a job.

The squirrels did their best
to build the kitten
into their act.

But he
couldn't quite
get the
hang of it . . .

That night, the kitten
didn't sleep well at all.

He felt as though
he'd let everyone down.

Maybe he would
have to go home.

Then, in the morning,
he had a teeny, tiny thought.

Big Top 'n' Tails Circus

free cheez

By midday,
it had grown
into a brainwave.

And, by evening, it had become
a **BIG IDEA**.

Bigger than any he'd ever had before.

BIG TOP 'N' TAILS CIRCUS

Word spread quicker than fleas on a ferret, and audiences flocked to the extraordinary animal circus.

ROLL UP!

BIG TOP 'N' TAILS CIRCUS

Because the kitten hadn't just thought *BIG*.

Oh, no. This time, he'd thought . . .

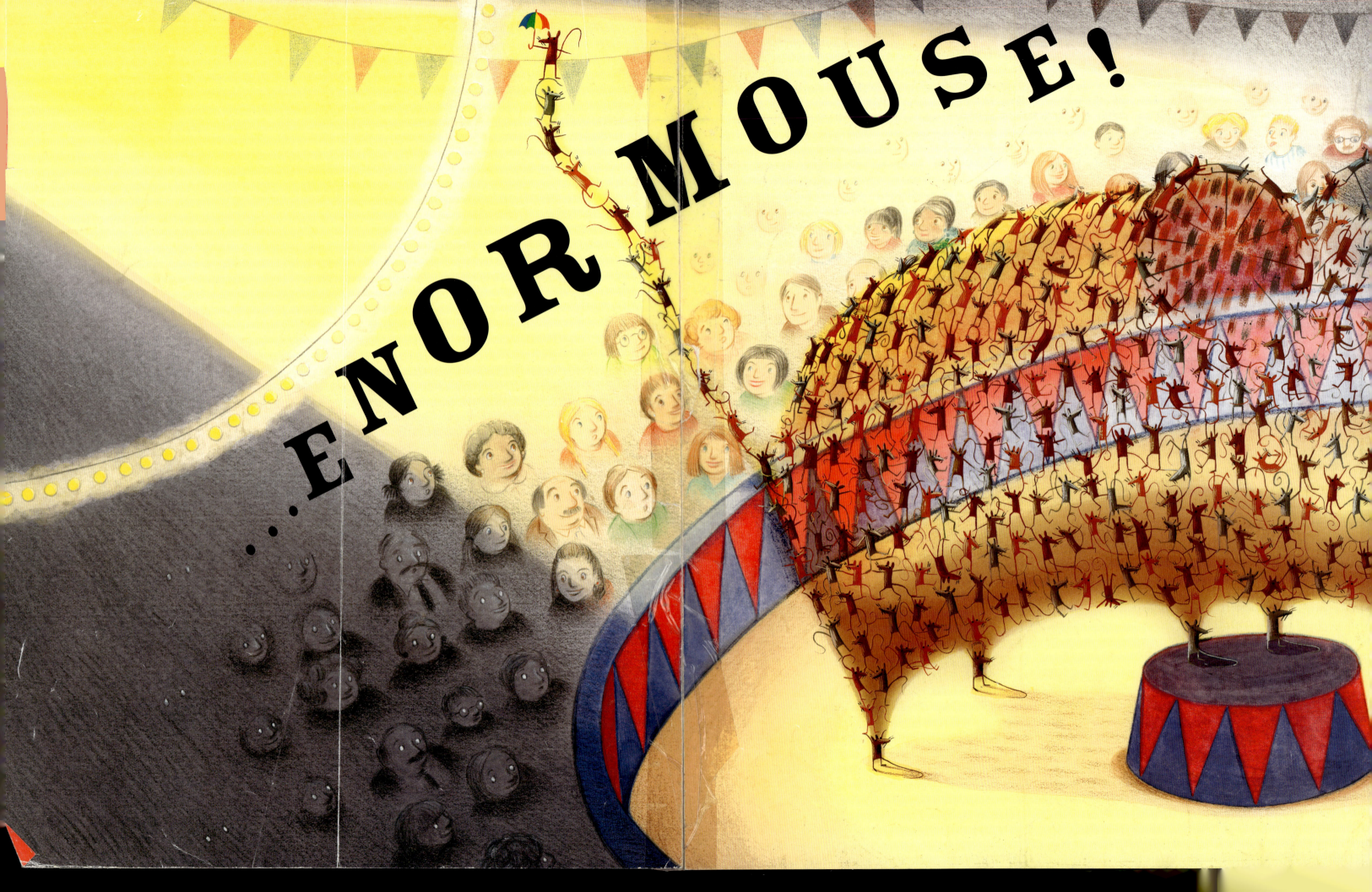

...ENORMOUSE!

The exciting *new act* travelled *f a r* and *w i d e*

MOSKVA

San Francisco

Paris

...be back soon.

Yours,

Miss Mitzy Ra-Ra II

The Furs

Mews Street

Kitford

Roma

(and back again).

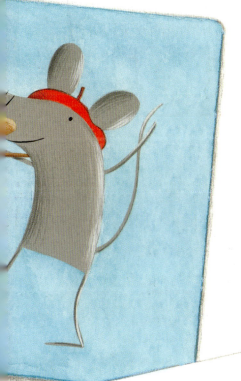

Wherever he went,
the kitten always
sent postcards to
his biggest fan.

Wish you
were here

Miss Mitzy Ra-Ra II

The Furs

And every single show was an absolute sell-out.

In fact, it was still pulling crowds long after the kitten had become a cat . . .

. . . and had
kittens of his own.

So remember,
the teeny, tiny things
are what make the
BIG things happen.

But, ladies
and gentlemen,
don't just think **BIG** —
think . . .